Weekly Reader Children's Book Club presents

Written and illustrated by

Bill Basso

DODD, MEAD & COMPANY
New York

Printed in the United States of America

1 2 3 4 5 6 7 8 9 10

Library of Congress Cataloging in Publication Data
Basso, Bill.
The Top of the Pizzas.
SUMMARY: An ugly pizza maker loses his job
because of his looks but finally finds work making
pizzas on the roof of an old skyscraper.
[1. Pizza—Fiction] I. Title.
PZ7.B2936To [Fic] 77-6085
ISBN 0-396-07463-4
Weekly Reader Children's Book Club Edition

To my wife and children

NOT TOO LONG AGO, in a place not too far away, there lived a good person who was as ugly as an ogre. And for that he was called Ogre. Ogre loved to make delicious pizza pies, and for that he was called Ogre Pizza-Ola.

Ogre worked at Leonardo's Pizzeria. Leonardo was the waiter and Ogre the chef. Leonardo knew Ogre to be a harmless and gentle soul, but because Ogre was so ugly, Leonardo kept him a secret. Poor Ogre had to make his pizzas in the rear of the kitchen where none of the customers were allowed. Leonardo thought if people knew about Ogre, they wouldn't buy his pizzas or allow their children in the pizzeria. When customers asked Leonardo, "Who is making these delicious pizzas," he would lie or change the subject. Leonardo kept his secret well.

Ogre made his pizzas just right—lots of molten mozzarella, anchovies, mushrooms, peppers, sausage, and gobs of rich tomato sauce. Leonardo's Pizzeria was the most popular place in town. Pizza lovers would travel for miles just for a slice. After school, crowds of happy children filled the pizzeria. Ogre especially loved the children, but he was sad he could not talk to them and tell them funny stories. Leonardo wouldn't allow it.

THE HOME OF
LEONARDO'S
PIZZA
PIZZA
LEONARDO'S PIZZERIA
PIZZA
TAXI

One fateful day, Mrs. Worthington Flaunt, the well-known hostess, insisted on meeting the chef who made the most delightful pizza she had ever tasted. "I must invite this pizza gourmet to my daughter's birthday sleep-over," she announced. Before Leonardo could stop her, Mrs. Flaunt was in the kitchen.

EMPLOYEES ONLY
KEEP
OUT

Mrs. Flaunt came out screaming, *"There's an ogre in the kitchen!"*

Leonardo's secret was no more. Parents panicked. They clutched their children and wisked them away as though they were escaping with their lives.

After that, no one came to the pizzeria again. Leonardo told Ogre he had to leave.

THE HOME OF
LE NARDO'S PIZ ERIA

And so, Ogre left town in search of a new job. He was very depressed. He had lost the only job he ever loved. Ogre went from pizzeria to pizzeria, but no one would hire him. He tried to explain his name. "I'm not really an ogre," he pleaded. "I never ate any child or pet." But no one would listen. Instead, they locked up their children and pets and hid in their homes. Ogre thought of changing his name, but that didn't matter—he still looked like an ogre.

Ogre was alone and hungry. He thought of what it was like to be a real ogre. He might as well be one—everyone believed he ate children and pets. But Ogre Pizza-Ola was a good person. He couldn't do that. If he could only get a job, any job.

One day in Big City, Ogre saw a sign on an old skyscraper. It read, "WANTED. ONE HARMLESS, TERRIBLE-LOOKING PERSON FOR HIRE. INQUIRE WITH SUPERINTENDENT." Ogre couldn't believe his eyes. At last a chance for a job.

The super told Ogre he needed him to take the place of a broken gargoyle.

"What's a gargoyle?" Ogre asked.

"A statue of a terrible-looking demon," answered the super. "A long time ago, people used to put them on the roofs of buildings to scare away real demons. Nobody believes that anymore. These days they just don't make gargoyles. Instead, I think you'll do nicely."

The kindly super told Ogre he wanted tourists to see his roof. "I want every detail in perfect order," he explained. "This building is the only one with gargoyles left in the city. Come with me. I'll show you what I mean."

SUPT.

Ogre followed the super up three thousand steps to the top of his building. The roof looked like a museum, and the view was the best in the city. The super thought many sightseers would pay to see such a place.

Ogre took the job and promised he would do his best.

It wasn't much of a job pretending to be a stone gargoyle. Poor Ogre sat on the ledge in all kinds of weather. He wondered if he would ever be a pizza chef again.

The super waited weeks for tourists to arrive. Only one exhausted family came. They complained about being too hungry and thirsty for sightseeing, and left.

ADMISSION
$1.50
BIG CITY

The super was upset. He didn't have any food or drink to sell. The super knew nothing about the food business. But Ogre Pizza-Ola did.

Ogre asked the super if he could make pizzas for the tourists. "A pizzeria on the roof?" thought the super. "I love it!" he exclaimed. "We'll call it 'The Top of the Pizzas.' What an attraction. A living gargoyle who makes pizzas." Of course Ogre didn't want to be an attraction. He wanted to be known and liked as a person, but Ogre was a pizza chef again and for that he was grateful.

It was opening day and Ogre was nervous. He remembered the time when Mrs. Flaunt came into his kitchen. This time Ogre was not hidden, but in the open where everyone could see him.

The first group to visit The Top of the Pizzas was a class of children and their teacher, Miss Crumpt. Miss Crumpt took one look at Ogre and saw his horns, his pointed ears, warts on his large nose—and fainted. The children looked at Ogre and saw something else. They saw kindness in his eyes, warmth in his smile, and heard his shy, gentle voice. The children were not afraid. They liked Ogre.

When Miss Crumpt was revived, she saw her class was safe. The children explained Ogre was harmless. Ogre's kind and gentle manner put Miss Crumpt at ease. Then the children gave her a slice of pizza. Well, she never tasted anything so delicious.

The class learned a lot this trip. They saw the city and enjoyed Ogre's pizzas and funny stories.

Soon after, the word spread about Ogre Pizza-Ola, and more and more curious tourists visited The Top of the Pizzas. No one seemed to mind Ogre's looks. As a matter of fact, everyone thought he blended beautifully with the scene.